THIS WALKER BOOK BELONGS TO:

_____

_____

_____

_____

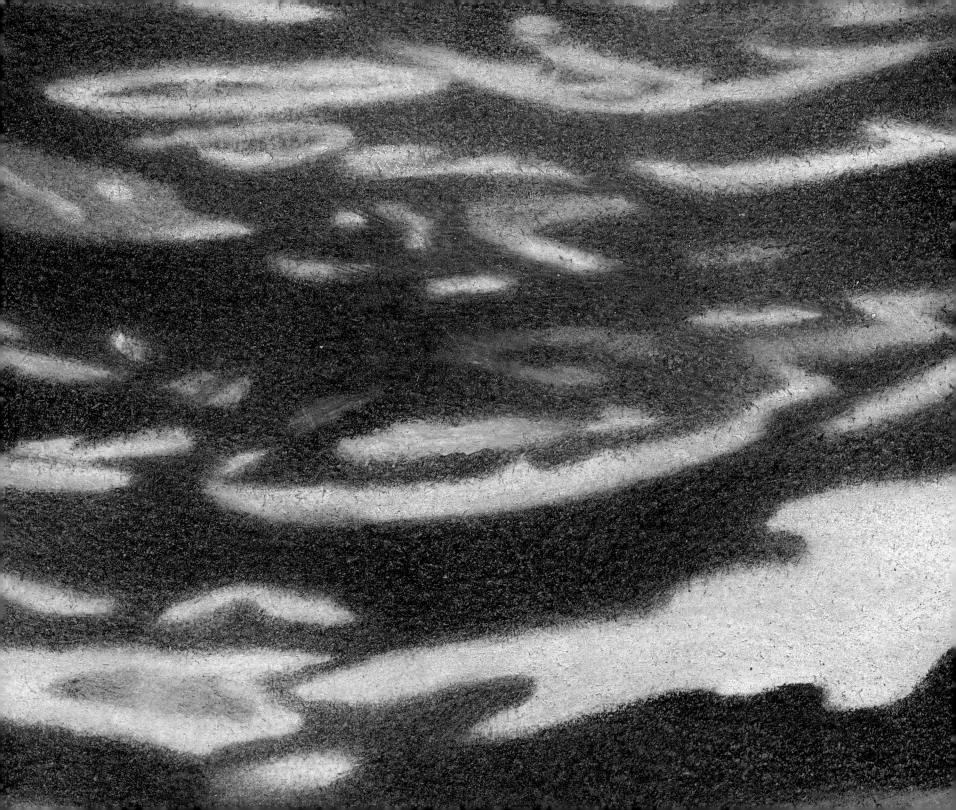

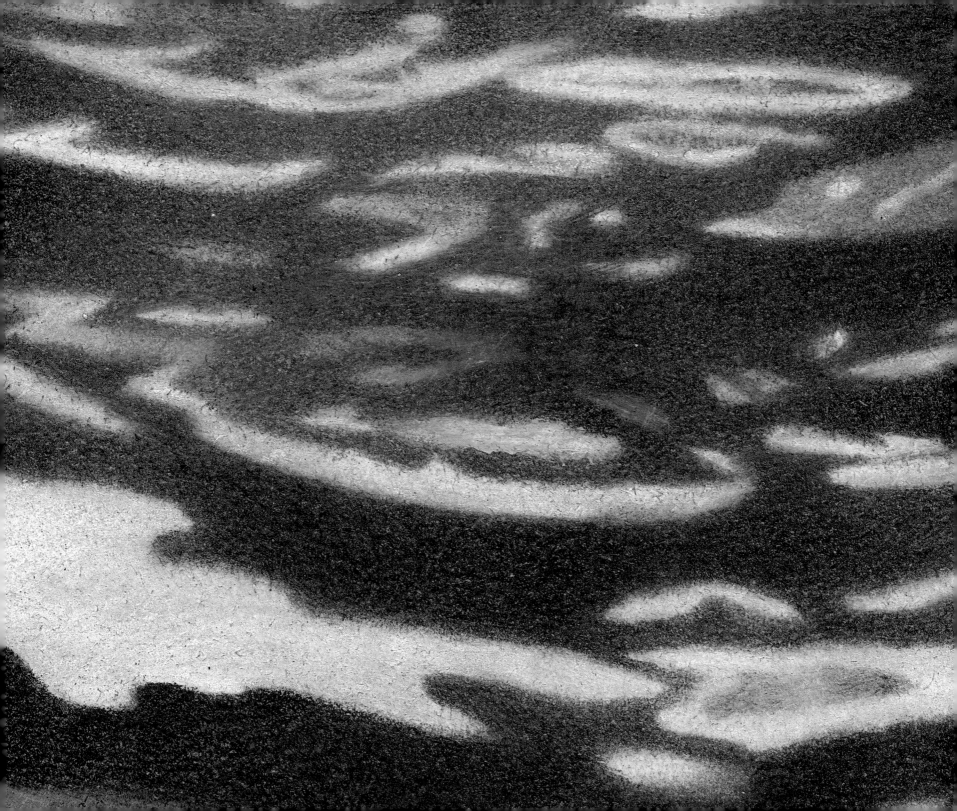

For D.L.
M.W.

For W.A.D.
J. E.

First published 1994 by Walker Books Ltd
87 Vauxhall Walk, London SE11 5HJ

This edition published 1996

10 9

Text © 1994 Martin Waddell
Illustrations © 1994 Jennifer Eachus

The right of Martin Waddell and Jennifer Eachus to be identified
as author and illustrator of this work has been asserted by them
in accordance with the Copyright, Designs and Patents Act 1988

This book has been typeset in Bauer Bodoni

Printed in Hong Kong

British Library Cataloguing in Publication Data:
a catalogue record for this book
is available from the British Library

ISBN 0-7445-4723-7

www.walkerbooks.co.uk

The Big Big Sea

Written by
MARTIN WADDELL

Illustrated by
JENNIFER EACHUS

WALKER BOOKS
AND SUBSIDIARIES
LONDON • BOSTON • SYDNEY

Mum said, "Let's go!"
So we went…

out of the house
and into the dark
and I saw…
THE MOON.

We went over the field
and under the fence
and I saw
the sea in the moonlight,
waiting for me.

And I ran
and Mum ran.
We ran and we ran
straight through the puddles
and out to the sea!

I went right in
to the shiny bit.
There was only me
in the big big sea.

I splashed
and I laughed
and Mum came after me
and we paddled
out deep in the water.

We got all wet.

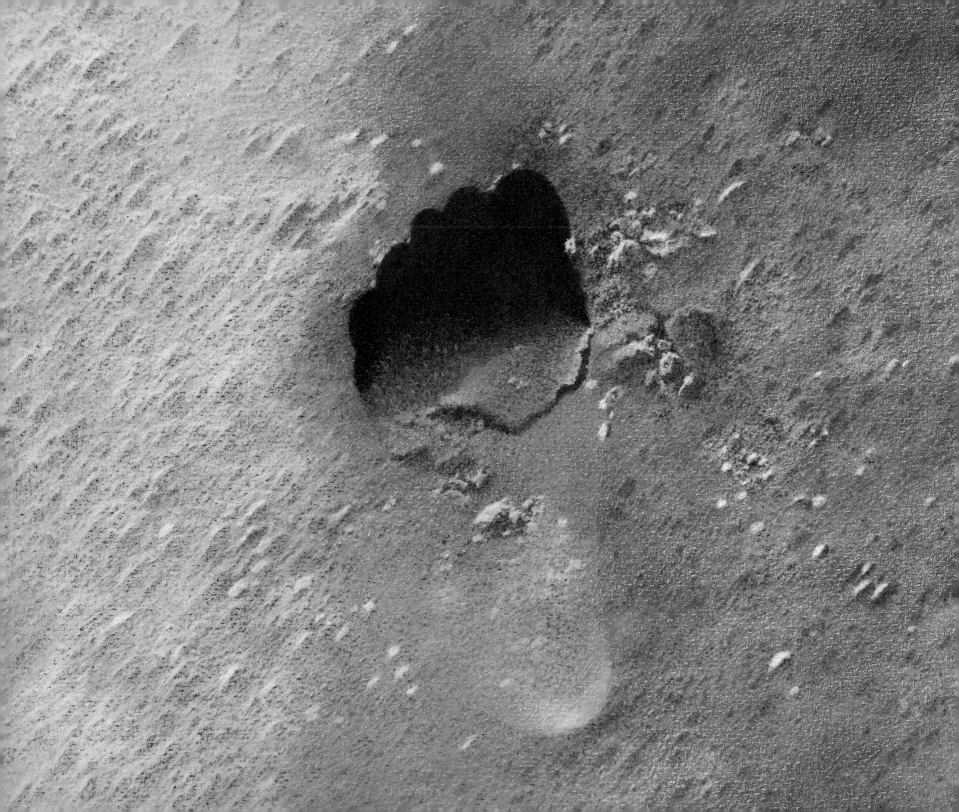

Then we walked
a bit more
by the edge of the sea
and our feet
made big holes
in the sand.

Far far away
right round the bay
were the town
and the lights
and the mountains.
We felt very small,
Mum and me.

We didn't go to the town.
We just stayed for a while
by the sea.

And Mum said to me,
"Remember this time.
It's the way life should be."

I got cold
and Mum carried me
all the way back.

We sat by the fire,
Mum and me,
and ate hot buttered toast
and I went to sleep
on her knee.

I'll always remember
just Mum and me
and the night
that we walked
by the big big sea.

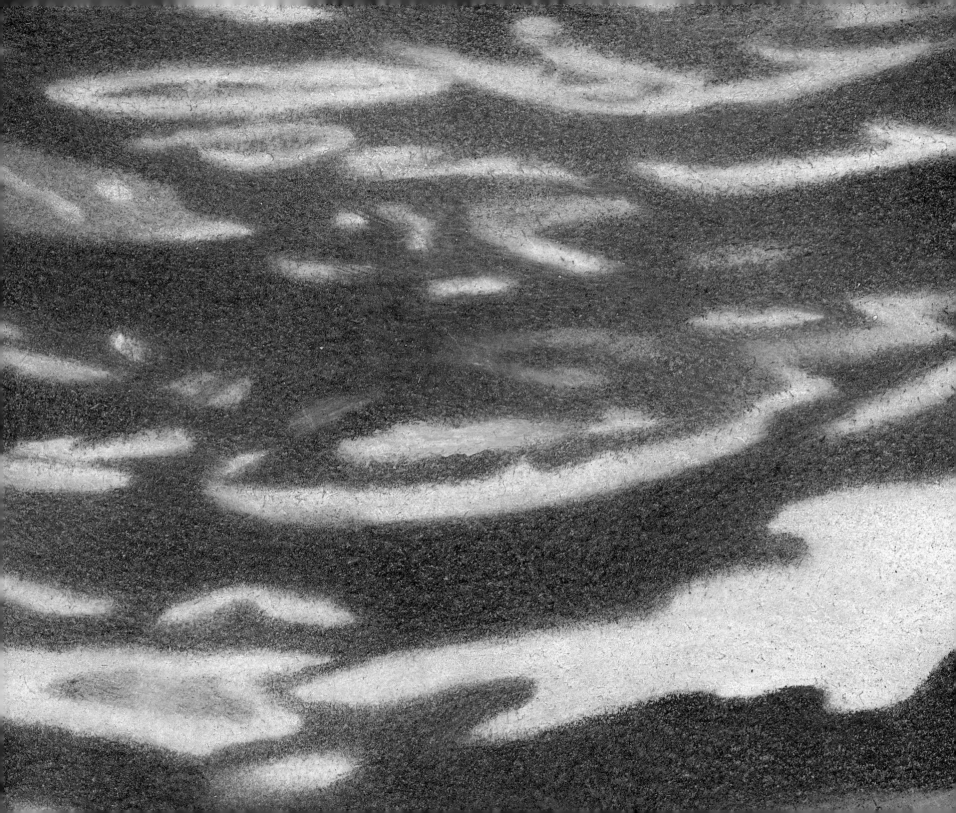

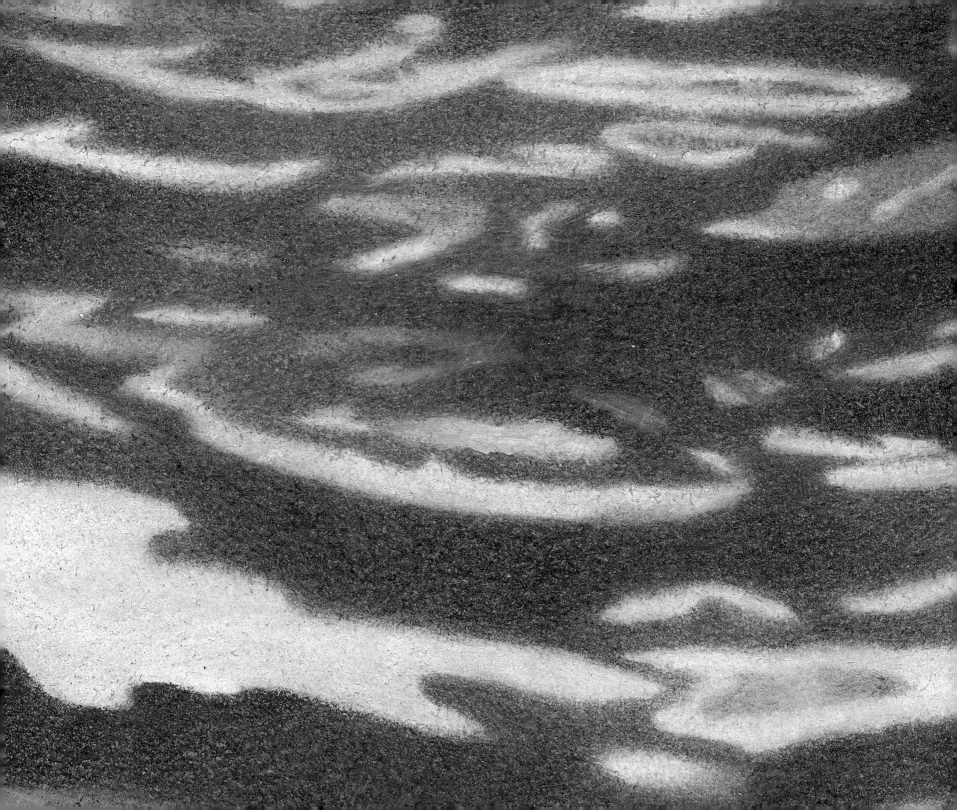